VISIT US AT
www.abdopublishing.com

Reinforced library bound edition published in 2010 by Spotlight, a division of the ABDO Group, 8000 West 78th Street, Edina, Minnesota 55439. Spotlight produces high-quality reinforced library bound editions for schools and libraries. Published by agreement with Warner Bros.—A Time Warner Company. All rights reserved. Used under authorization.

Printed in the United States of America, Melrose Park, Illinois.
092009
012010

 PRINTED ON RECYCLED PAPER

Library of Congress Cataloging-in-Publication Data

Simmons, Alex.
  Scooby-Doo in Dead & let spy / writer, Alex Simmons ; penciller, Robert Pope ; inker, Scott McRae ; colorist, Heroic Age ; letterer, Travis Lanham. -- Reinforced library bound ed.
     p. cm. -- (Scooby-Doo graphic novels)
  ISBN 978-1-59961-692-6
  1. Graphic novels. I. Pope, Robert. II. Scooby-Doo (Television program) III. Title. IV. Title: Scooby-Doo in Dead and let spy. V. Title: Dead & let spy.
  PZ7.7.S49Sc 2010
  741.5'973--dc22

                              2009032897

All Spotlight books have reinforced library bindings and
are manufactured in the United States of America.

GRRR

FWOOOSH

OOOF!!!

ARRRRGH!

ORRRRRG!!

OOOOOOO?

THOUGHT THEY HAD YOU *THAT* TIME.

NO... NOT *YETI*.

DEAD & LET SPY

Writer: ALEX SIMMONS
Penciller: ROBERT POPE
Inker: SCOTT MCRAE
Colorist: HEROIC AGE
Letterer: TRAVIS LANHAM
Editor: MICHAEL SIGLAIN

WUMP WUMP WUMP

WOOSH

THAT IS BANG.

IT SURE WAS A *BANG*, BUT--

NO. I MEANT THAT TEEN AGENT IS *J.Z. BANG*, MY NEPHEW. THIS FOOTAGE WAS SHOT BY SOME OF PROFESSOR BITS' SPY-CAMS.

J.Z. IS ONE OF THE YOUNGEST AND BEST AGENTS WE HAVE.

HE IS ALSO THE MOST *RECKLESS*, IRRESPONSIBLE--

WHERE IS J.Z. NOW?

CAN'T TELL YOU.

WHAT'S THE MISSION?

CAN'T TELL YOU.

BECAUSE IT'S TOP SECRET?

NO...BECAUSE I DON'T KNOW. J.Z. RECEIVES HIS ORDERS DIRECTLY FROM THE SOURCE. HE'S BEEN RUNNING SOLO ON THIS MISSION.

AND HE WRECKS EVERY PIECE OF EQUIPMENT I GIVE HIM!

THIS IS PROFESSOR BITS.

HE'S THE GADGET GURU WHO DESIGNS ALL OUR SPECIAL EQUIPMENT.

HE NEVER LISTENS WHEN I TRY TO INSTRUCT HIM ON--

ALL I CAN TELL YOU IS J.Z. CLAIMS HE'S BEING CHASED BY GHOSTS AND GHOULS. WE THOUGHT IT MIGHT BE THE WORK OF A FREELANCE AGENT CALLED *CADAVER.*

HE LOOKS LIKE A *CORPSE.*

HE GATHERS INFORMATION AND SELLS IT TO THE HIGHEST BIDDER. CADAVER USES SPOOKY TRICKS TO GET THE INFORMATION.

ARE YOU SURE THEY'RE *TRICKS?*

ALL I KNOW IS THAT MY NEPHEW NEEDS YOUR HELP-- SO WE'RE SENDING YOU IN.

WILL WE GET A TRICK CAR AND BRIEFCASE, AND--

ALL I CAN GIVE YOU IS A NUMBER FOR J.Z.'S COMMUNICATOR.

HE'LL EXPLAIN EVERYTHING ELSE...

"...WHEREVER HE AGREES TO MEET YOU."

WHEN UNCLE G SAID HE WAS CALLING IN M.I.-5, I DIDN'T KNOW HE MEANT YOU FIVE FROM *MYSTERY INC.*

BUT THANKS FOR JUMPIN' ON BOARD AT THE LAST MINUTE.

THAT'S OUR SPECIALTY. NOW WHAT'S UP?

I RECEIVED A SECRET MESSAGE FROM DOCTOR OOH--

OH.

NO, *OOH!*

OH. OOH.

DOCTOR *OOH* HAS INVENTED A DEVICE THAT HE WANTS THE U.S. TO HAVE.

WHAT'S IT DO?

I CAN'T TELL YOU.

OH.

NO, OOH. ANYWAY, THE DOCTOR'S MESSAGE SAID HE'D ONLY TURN IT OVER TO ME.

WHY?

BEFORE HE BECAME A SCIENTIFIC *GENIUS*, HE WAS AN *ECCENTRIC* SCIENCE *TEACHER* AT MY HIGH SCHOOL.

TO PROTECT HIS DEVICE, HE DIVIDED IT INTO SEVERAL PARTS, AND HID THEM IN DIFFERENT AREAS OF THE WORLD. HIS SECRET MESSAGES TELL ME THE LOCATIONS.

ONLY PROBLEM IS EVERY TIME I GO TO GET ONE OF THEM, I RUN INTO CREEPS FROM A LATE-NIGHT *HORROR FEST.*

I'VE GOT FIVE MORE PARTS TO GO.

YOU'RE A SECRET AGENT--CAN'T YOU USE YOUR GADGETS AND KARATE AND--

SURE, BUT I... I...

NEVER MIND, J.Z. THAT'S WHY *WE'RE* HERE.

YES, YOU HANDLE THE *SPY* STUFF, AND WE'LL TAKE CARE OF THE *SPOOKY* STUFF.

ZOINKS! LIKE, COULD WE SWITCH THAT AROUND?

THIS WAY TO THE BAGGAGE CAR!

WHAT ABOUT THE NEXT PART OF THE PROFESSOR'S INVENTION?

VELMA... TANKS FOR REMINDING ME!

JINKIES! WE'RE TRAPPED.

OH YEAH?

JZB

WHERE DID YOU GET THIS?

I, UH, BORROWED IT FROM PROFESSOR BITS... SORT OF.

B-KRG

SWOOSH

LIKE, YOU SURE GOT US OUT OF THAT!

BUT YOU FROZE FOR A MOMENT. WHAT'S WRONG, J.Z.?

IT'S A LONG STORY...

"WHEN I WAS A KID, MY FOLKS LOVED TO WATCH OLD MONSTER MOVIES.

"THEY REALLY SCARED ME.

"ESPECIALLY WHEN I WENT TO BED.

"BUT I DIDN'T TELL ANYONE. I DIDN'T WANT MY PARENTS AND FRIENDS TO THINK I WAS A SCAREDY CAT."

DID YOU EVER TELL YOUR UNCLE?

YEAH, BUT HE THINKS I'M OVER IT. TEEN SPIES *CAN'T* BE SCARED OF THE *BOGEYMAN.*

PROFESSOR BITS, IT'S J.Z. ARRANGE A PICK UP--

J.Z., WHERE ARE YOU? DID YOU TAKE--?

LOCATION 6, AND YES. YOU CAN PICK UP YOUR SPY-MOBILE THERE.

WHO KNEW WE WERE ON THE TRAIN?

NO ONE. I CAN'T TAKE A CHANCE OF A LEAK.

NOW THEN, WE'VE GOT 4 MORE PARTS TO PICK UP, AND THEY'RE ALL OVER THE GLOBE.

THEN LET'S GET GOING, MAYBE WE CAN HELP YOU GET THEM...

...AND THE LEADER OF THIS GHOUL SQUAD.

THIS IS THE LAST STOP. WE'RE *SUPPOSED* TO MEET DR. OOH HERE AND GET THE LAST PART OF THE DEVICE. BUT I...I DOUBT IT.

WHY?

BECAUSE THE DOCTOR DOESN'T LIKE WEIRD STUFF ANY MORE THAN I DO. SO WHY WOULD HE PICK THIS PLACE?

ROY & AL'S CASINO

THAT'S NOT THE *ONLY* THING THAT'S WEIRD AROUND HERE.

ZOINKS! DASH AND SCREAM TIME!

J.Z., ASK YOURSELF, IF THE LOCATIONS ARE SECRET, HOW DO THESE CREATURES ALWAYS KNOW WHERE TO FIND YOU?

OR, HAVE YOU NOTICED THAT THERE WERE SPY CAMERAS PLANTED ALMOST EVERYWHERE WE RAN INTO THE MONSTERS?

JINKIES, AND IN A WORLD OF SPIES AND HI-TECH GADGETS, WHY GHOSTS AND GOBLINS?

TO...TO PLAY ON MY CHILDHOOD FEARS!

RIGHT! AND SOMEONE HAD TO TELL THEM ABOUT THOSE FEARS. AND IF IT'S NOT YOUR UNCLE, THEN IT WOULD HAVE TO BE--

SOMEONE AT HQ!

TIME TO PLAY DEAD MAN'S HAND!

THE ONLY THING THAT'S *DYING* AROUND HERE IS YOUR ACT, ASTRO TURF!

BUT!

TIME TO SHED THE SHAG...

PROFESSOR!

IT'S NOT FAIR! NOT *FAIR!!!*

WE SENT FOR YOUR UNCLE WHEN WE REALIZED THIS WHOLE MISSION WAS A SETUP.

WHY, BITS?

BECAUSE I COULDN'T TAKE IT ANYMORE! YOUR NEPHEW IS SOOOOO RECKLESS!

HE'S LOST THREE SOLO COPTERS, CRASHED FIVE ALL-TERRAIN VEHICLES, AND SOAKED NINE OF MY MINI-MIKES IN VARIOUS CHIP DIPS!

YOU EVEN DESTROYED MY *INDESTRUCTIBLE* SUIT!

HOW DID I KNOW IT WASN'T MACHINE WASHABLE?

I WANTED YOU GONE TO SAVE MY INVENTIONS! SO WHEN I FOUND OUT ABOUT YOUR PHOBIA, I KNEW WHAT I HAD TO DO!

OH, MY PRECIOUS CREATIONS, MY BEAUTIES, MY *BUDGET...*

I THINK BITS NEEDS SOME DOWN TIME. THERE'S A LITTLE VILLAGE I COULD SEND HIM TO.

I ALMOST BLEW THE MISSION.

BUT YOU DIDN'T, J.Z. YOU OVERCAME YOUR FEARS-- FOR REAL THIS TIME.

YEAH, WELL, I COULDN'T HAVE DONE IT WITHOUT M.I.-5 HERE.

HOW CAN I THANK YOU?

GET YOUR UNCLE TO SPRING FOR TWO OF THE BIGGEST BANQUETS A SUPER SPY EVER HAD! RIGHT, SCOOB?

RAKE RAT ROO RANRETS!

LIKE, WHY NOT? YOU ONLY *EAT* TWICE!

THE END

HEY! A BELLY-BUSTIN' BURGER JOINT! LIKE, I'M STARVING!

REE ROO!

NOT A CHANCE. YOU'RE GOING TO EAT HEALTHY FOR ONCE.

ZOINKS!

AAAAAAAHHH!!!

WHERE'D HE COME FROM?

RIGHT RERE!

THAT FRUIT STAND! LIKE, WHAT WERE YOU SAYING ABOUT HEALTHY EATING?

SHAGGY, THERE IS *NOTHING* WRONG WITH EITHER FRUIT OR THAT FRUIT STAND.

SURE THERE IS-- *COOKIES* TASTE BETTER AND THAT PLACE IS, LIKE, *HAUNTED!*

DON'T BE SILLY. THAT FRUIT IS NOT--

AA-AAAAAAAAAHH!!!

YOU WERE SAYING?

The GHOSTLY FRUIT STAND

SCOTT PETERSON-Writer   VINCE DEPORTER-Artist
HEROIC AGE-Colorist   NICK J. NAPOLITANO-Letterer
MICHAEL SIGLAIN-Editor

THE END

SHAGGY AND SCOOBY-DOO ARE SUPPOSED TO INVESTIGATE THIS *CREEPY CASTLE*, BUT SCATTERED THROUGHOUT THE SCENE ARE 16 THINGS SHAG AND SCOOB ARE *DEATHLY* AFRAID OF. CAN YOU HELP THEM FIND ALL OF THE *HORRORS* THAT HAUNT THIS *SPOOKY CASTLE*?

PICTURE this MYSTERY

SCOTT CUNNINGHAM-Writer   JOE STATON-Penciller   JEFF ALBRECHT-Inker
HEROIC AGE-Colorist   NICK J. NAPOLITANO-Letterer   MICHAEL SIGLAIN-Editor

VAMPIRE BAT, SKELETON, MEDIEVAL AXE, CROCODILE, PYTHON, BLOODY SWORD, SPIDER, SPIKED MACE CLUB, GHOST, HAUNTED ARMOR, RAT, BUBBLING CAULDRON, MAN-EATING SHARK, CANNON, COFFIN & BROCCOLI.

The DRAGON in the BATHROOM

Writer - SCOTT PETERSON
Artist - VINCE DEPORTER
Colorist - HEROIC AGE
Letterer - NICK J. NAPOLITANO
Editor - MICHAEL SIGLAIN

CONDEMNED!

WELL, I'M GOING TO CHECK IT OUT.

I'M WITH YOU, DAPHNE.

LIKE, US TOO. WE'RE RIGHT BEHIND YOU.

RAY, RAY REHIND ROO.

RAGGY...

I KNOW, PAL. MAYBE FIVE GIGANTO-GULPS WAS TOO MANY.

OH MAN... WHY CAN'T WE EVER BREAK DOWN IN FRONT OF A NICE NEW DONUT SHOP?

NOT EXACTLY HOMEY, IS IT?

RO ROY.

WELL, I REALLY GOTTA GO, SO...HERE GOES NOTHIN'.

RELL?

LIKE, DON'T RUSH ME.

CLICK

WELL, HERE IT IS. WHO'S GOING FIRST?

I DON'T WANNA... BUT I GOTTA.

OKAY. I'M HERE. THERE'S, LIKE, NOTHING TO BE AFRAID OF.

RIGHT.

AAAAAAAAHHH!!!

SCOOB! YOU SCARED ME WITLESS!

RORRY.

AH... S'OKAY, PAL. KINDA NICE TO HAVE COMPANY.

BUT, LIKE, NOT TOO MUCH COMPANY!

DO YOU HEAR THAT *HISSING?*

AND SEE THOSE *EYES?*

RES!

RAGONS!

FIRE EYES! RUN!

WAIT A MINUTE. ARE YOU TALKING ABOUT THAT *HISSING?*

REAH! RAGON REATH!

THAT'S JUST *AIR BUBBLES* IN THE *WATER PIPES.*

AND THE *EYES* WERE JUST THE *FLASHLIGHTS* REFLECTED IN THE *MIRROR.*

ROOPS. REE-HEE!

RELIEVED?

NOT YET-- NOW I GOTTA GO WORSE THAN EVER!

REE ROO!

THE END

DANGER-PRONE DAPHNE

ALEX SIMMONS-WRITER
JOE STATON-PENCILLER • **JEFF ALBRECHT**-INKER
HEROIC AGE-COLORIST • **NICK J. NAPOLITANO**-LETTERER
MICHAEL SIGLAIN-EDITOR

SO YOU'VE COME TO RESCUE THE ROJAS FAMILY, AND CAPTURE ME, THE *PT GIEST?*

BUT TSK, TSK...FOUR DOWN, ONE TO GO.

AND I'LL GET YOU TOO, MY *PRETTY!*

WHY ARE YOU *HAUNTING* THIS HOUSE? WHAT DO YOU WAN--!

WHAT I *HAVE*-- YOU AND YOUR FRIENDS IN MY *CLUTCHES!*

TRAPPING YOU ALL WASN'T MUCH OF A CHALLENGE, NOT FOR A *GENIUS* LIKE ME.

BUT I'LL GIVE YOU A *SPORTING* CHANCE.